My Granny Loves
HOCKEY

Lori Weber with illustrations by *Eliska Liska*

SIMPLY READ BOOKS

Published in 2014 by Simply Read Books
www.simplyreadbooks.com

Text © 2014 Lori Weber
Illustrations © 2014 Eliska Liska

Library and Archives Canada Cataloguing in Publication

Weber, Lori, 1959-, author
    My granny loves hockey / written by Lori Weber ; illustrated
by Eliska Liska.

ISBN 978-1-927018-43-9

    I. Liska, Eliska, 1981-, illustrator II. Title.

PS8645.E24M9 2014   jC813'.6   C2013-906057-X

We gratefully acknowledge for their financial support of our publishing program the
Canada Council for the Arts, the BC Arts Council, and the Government of Canada
through the Canada Book Fund (CBF).

Manufactured in Malaysia

Book design by Robin Mitchell Cranfield for hundreds & thousands

10 9 8 7 6 5 4 3 2 1

*To Isaac, Josh, and Cassidy — three wonderful grandchildren
who help me shout, "Go, Habs, GO!" — LW*

*For the best grandmas: Babicka Vlasta and Lida, and the new ones Baba Blaza
and Baba Bobbie! — EL*

On Saturday nights, Granny and I watch hockey. I wheel Granny close to the screen. That way, she can follow the puck as it whips around the rink.

When someone scores, Granny and I shout **hooray!**

"Did you play hockey when you were little?" I ask Granny.

"When I was little, girls were not allowed to play hockey," she says.

"Why not?"

"It was only for boys."

"What did girls do?"

"They learned how to make soup and clean and sew."

"Were they allowed to watch hockey on television?" I ask.

Granny laughs. "There was no television back then, honey," she says.

"What was there?"

"There was only the rink on the lake behind our house. It froze all the way across, to where the pine forest stood."

"Could you watch hockey there?" I ask.

"Oh, yes. I watched my brothers play," Granny says, looking sad. "But I wanted so badly to join them. Instead, I had to go home and help my mother."

"So you never got to play?"

"No, sweetie. I only played hockey in *my dreams*."

Sometimes, I take Granny outside so that she can feel the sun on her cheeks. We stop to listen to birds chirp or to pet friendly cats. When it snows, we make snowballs to throw at street signs.

Sometimes, Granny holds my *hockey stick*, flicking snow as we roll along. If kids are playing hockey at the park, we stop and watch them.

"That kid needs to loosen up," Granny says.
The goalie is standing stiff as a statue in front of the net.

"That kid sure can stick-handle," Granny says. A boy is zooming
across the rink, popping the puck between people's skates then
scooping it up again with the tip of his stick.

"And that girl has to bend her knees more," Granny says.
A girl is trying to skate backwards, but getting nowhere.

"Now, let's see what you can do," Granny says.
I lace up *my skates* and take my stick from Granny's lap.

I skate into the game and pass the *puck* to a kid near the *net.*
He shoots, but the goalie kicks out her leg and stops it.

"Nice try," Granny calls out.

The next time the puck comes to me I hit it between a kid's legs, then
sneak around him to get it back. I skate toward the net, sliding the
puck back and forth, until a bigger kid steals it from me.

"You're getting better all the time," shouts Granny.

I can't play for long because Granny gets cold. I tuck her blanket around her lap and we head home. On the way, Granny falls fast asleep.

One day, Mom and I take Granny to the doctor for a check-up. I am not allowed into the examination room.

When Mom comes out, she says, "The doctor says there is nothing wrong with Granny. She is just old and old people get tired."

The next time Granny wants me to wheel her to the *rink*, I say, "Mom said you have to take it easy."

"Easy, schmeazy! What does that mean? I may be old, but I'm not ready to start knitting booties," Granny says. "Now, take me to that rink."

So I do.

Granny makes me push her right up to the edge of the rink. When she stares at the ice, her eyes go far far away. It's like she is seeing a picture that is deep inside her head.

That's when I get an idea.

"Hey, everyone! Come here," I call, waving my hands. All the kids stop playing and skate over.

"I need your help," I say. "Granny wants to play."

Nobody laughs. They look down at Granny, who is holding my stick like a pro.

"Help me slide her onto the ice."

Granny's eyes shine brightly as we wheel her toward the net. When we stop, Granny slaps her stick onto the ice. I drop the puck beside it. We turn her sideways.

Granny's eyes lock on the goalie. She is looking for empty spaces between the goalie's pads or over her shoulders. Then Granny pulls back her stick and shoots, snapping the puck into the air. We hold our breath as we watch the puck sail past the goalie's glove.

"**Hooray**," we all shout, clapping our sticks on the ice. "Granny scored!"

"What a shot," yells the goalie.

Granny's smile is wider than the net.

Granny falls asleep on the way home, her wrinkled eyelids shut tight. Her mouth twitches and her arms jerk, and I know she's dreaming.

She is skating, pushing the puck across the frozen lake. Her brothers lag behind, pumping their legs as they try to catch her. Way behind them, her mother is waving, calling her home to do some chores.

Granny doesn't stop. Her hair is flying in the wind. She whacks the puck, making a cracking sound that echoes around the lake. The puck lifts into the air, sailing way up, over the tops of the trees and into the pine forest.

"**Hooray**," I shout, throwing my arms into the air.
"Two *great shots* in one day."

"It was easy," Granny replies, waking up.

She winks at me and I wheel her the rest of the way home.